# You Read to Me, I'll Read to You

## Very Short Scary Tales to Read Together

**by**

MARY ANN HOBERMAN

**Illustrated by**

MICHAEL EMBERLEY

Megan Tingley Books

LITTLE, BROWN AND COMPANY

Books for Young Readers

New York   Boston

*To M.E. "How about some monster stories?"*
—M.A.H.

*To M.A.H. For indulging me.*
—M.E.

Little, Brown and Company

Hachette Book Group
1290 Avenue of the Americas, New York, NY 10104
Visit our website at lb-kids.com

Little, Brown and Company is a division of Hachette Book Group, Inc.
The Little, Brown name and logo are trademarks of Hachette Book Group, Inc.

The publisher is not responsible for websites (or their content)
that are not owned by the publisher.

First Paperback Edition: August 2009

Library of Congress Cataloging-in-Publication Data
Hoberman, Mary Ann.
You read to me, I'll read to you very scary tales to read together /
by Mary Ann Hoberman ; illustrated by Michael Emberley. — 1st ed.
p. cm.
ISBN: 978-0-316-01733-6 (hc) / ISBN: 978-0-316-04351-9 (pb)
1. Children's poetry, American. I. Emberley, Michael. II. Title.
PS3558.O3367Y68 2006
811'.54 — dc22

2006001223

10 9

APS

Printed in China

The illustrations for this book were done in pencil, watercolor, and dry pastel
on 90-lb. hot-press watercolor paper.
The text and display type is set in Shannon.

# Table Of Contents

## Author's Note:

Here is another read-together/read-aloud book, *Scary Tales*, the fourth in the YOU READ TO ME, I'LL READ TO YOU series. This time monsters and their ilk provide the subject matter, and once again the text itself indicates who reads what when. But unlike the previous two books, which presented playful versions of familiar fairy tales and nursery rhymes, this one makes up brand-new stories about many of the scary creatures children delight in.

This book, like the others, is for readers of all stages and ages: pairs of beginning readers, young or old or young *and* old, as well as pairs made up of a beginner and a more-advanced reader. The book also lends itself to choral readings. And of course readers can always switch parts and colors and read the stories again, so that they all get a chance to play all the characters!

I continue to acknowledge the admirable work of Literacy Volunteers of America and all the other dedicated literacy tutors who continue to offer the precious gift of reading to students young and old.

# Introduction

Do you like to
Quake and quiver?

Do you like to
Shake and shiver?

Do you like your
Mind all jumpy?

Do you like your
Skin all bumpy?

If you do,
Then take a look
At the stories
In this book!

I'll read here
And you'll read there.

Both sides give you
Quite a scare.

Then, with middle
Words before us,
Read together
In a chorus.
Now we know
Just what to do:

You'll read to me!

I'll read to you!

# The Mummy

Let's explore inside this tomb.

    I'm afraid we'll meet our doom.

Nothing's here to be afraid of.

    Here's a package! What's it made of?

Wow! I think it is a mummy!

    Butterflies are in my tummy.

It can't hurt you. Don't be scared.

    I would touch it if I dared.

Maybe we can both unwrap it.

    First I think we'd better tap it.
    What if someone's still inside?

You know mummies all have died.

    This unwrapping is a bother.

Maybe it was someone's father.

    Someone's dad? Don't be a dummy!

Maybe it was someone's mummy!

It's an awful lot of cloth.

**Eek! Let's go! I saw a moth!**

Come on, help me to unwind.

**I'm afraid of what we'll find.**

We'll be finished in a minute.

Leaping lizards! Nothing's in it!

All that trouble to unroll it.

**Then to find out someone stole it.**

Robbed its tomb. It makes me sick!

**Someone played a dirty trick!**

I would like to know who did it

**And to find out where they hid it.**

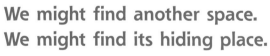

I think we should search some more.
Maybe there's a secret door.

**We might find another space.**
**We might find its hiding place.**

Wouldn't it be really yummy
If at last we found the mummy?
Maybe this book has a clue.
You'll read to me, I'll read to you.

7

# The Witch and the Broomstick

I'm a witch,
A wicked witch.
My hat and cape
Are black as pitch.

I'm the broomstick
That she flies on.
I'm the broomstick
She relies on.

When I fly
Above the town,
They look up
And I look down.

When I fly,
They all cry, "Whee!
Is that a broomstick
That we see?"

My nose is pointed.
So's my chin.
I'm skin and bones.
I'm very thin.
I am so skinny
I look sick.

I'm even thinner.
I'm a stick!

On Hallowe'en
I fly all night
And give the people
Quite a fright.

I take her high
Up in the sky.
Without my help
She couldn't fly.

And when I land
And stand up tall,
"Come see the witch!"
The people call.

And when I land
And off she slides,
The people come
And beg for rides.

And when it's time
For me to go,
The people weep.
They love me so.

That silly witch!
She doesn't see
That all her power
Comes from me!

That blockhead!
What's it thinking of?
I'm the one
That people love!

But while we squabble
And we spat,
We're stuck together.
That is that.
So let's make up
And start anew.
You read to me.
I'll read to you.

# The Dinosaur

Who's that knocking at my door?
Look, it is a dinosaur!

> How do you do? How have you been?
> Long time no see. May I come in?

My goodness! How did you arrive?
I didn't think you were alive!

> They say I am extinct, I know;
> But here I am. Just call me Joe.

I really can't believe my eyes!
I really can't believe your size!

> Please may I take a little rest?
> I promise I'll behave my best.

Oh dear, I fear you will not fit.
There's not a spot where you can sit.

> Then may I take a little snooze?
> I promise I'll take off my shoes.

My bed is far too small for you.
It's plain to see it will not do.

> Oh well, if I can't use your bed,
> I'll sit upon your roof instead.

My little house is not a chair.
Please use that mountain over there.

I thought you would be glad to see
Tyrannosaurus Rex. (That's me.)

I am. I really like your looks;
But you belong inside of books.

When I'm in books, I am not pleased.
Inside of books I'm really squeezed.
Outside of books I'm full of cheer.
I wish you'd let me settle here.

Well, if you settle in my yard,
Then you can be my bodyguard.

A good idea! I'll hide in trees
And scare away your enemies.

My friends will not believe it's true
I've got a bodyguard like you.

And then when bedtime comes around,
We'll both lie down upon the ground.

I'll take a book down from my shelf
And read you tales about yourself.

That will be nice. I'll read them, too.

You'll read to me! I'll read to you!

# Goblins, Gremlins, Demons, and Devils

There are goblins in the garden.

       **There are gremlins in the glen.**

There are demons in the cellar.

       **There are devils in the den.**

They are crawling in the windows.

       **They are creeping in the doors.**

They are sliding down the chimney.

       **They are slipping through the floors.**

Oh, we wish we knew some magic
That would get us out of here,
Or a secret spell to corner them
And make them disappear!

They are sneaking in my sneakers.

       **They are peeking in my nose.**

They are gnawing on my fingers.

       **They are nibbling at my toes.**

They are poking in my pockets.

       **They are hiding in my hair.**

They are climbing up my sweater.

       **They are in my underwear!**

There is no way to escape them!
They are high and they are low.
Will they pester us forever?
Will they never let us go?

Maybe we can think of something,

Something that they really need.

I don't notice any books here.

Do you think that they can read?

If we read a bedtime story

And it puts them all to sleep,

We'll slip out while they are sleeping;

But we mustn't make a peep.

We are glad we brought a book along
With scary stories, too!
You read a little bit to me
And then I'll read to you.

# The Skeleton

I think it would be lots of fun
To own a bony skeleton.

        A skeleton made out of bone?
        Why, what a splendid thing to own!

I would love it!

        I would, too!

      Think of all the things we'd do!

I'd hang it high up in the hall.
When someone came, I'd make it fall.

        I'd tie a bonnet on its head
        And lay it on my sister's bed

Or put on diapers and a bib
And hide it in the baby's crib

        Or dress it in my father's pants
        And hold it up so it could dance.

      We'd take it marching down the street
      And shake its bones to keep the beat

Or bury it inside a pit
And make our friends discover it

      Or maybe take it to the park
      And scare the people in the dark

Or we could sneak it into school
And play a joke for April Fool!

      And when our teacher wasn't there,
      We'd go and put it in her chair.

We'd dress it in her hat and coat
And tie a scarf around its throat;

      And then when she came back to look,
      We'd each be buried in a book.

We'd act surprised as anyone.
We'd say, "That's not our skeleton!"

      She wouldn't guess a thing, you see.
      I'd read to you. You'd read to me.

15

# The Ghost and the Mouse

I am a ghost.

      I am a mouse.

We live together
In this house.

      There's just one thing
      That's wrong, you see.

I'm scared of you.
You're scared of me.

      You're scared of me.
      I'm scared of you.

We know it's silly
But it's true.

      I'm scared of ghosts.

I'm scared of mice.

To live together
Isn't nice.

Each time I see a mouse,
I shriek.

      Each time I see a ghost,
      I squeak.

I wish that you
Would move away.

      I wish that you would move.
      I'll stay.

My grandma told me
Mice have germs.

        My grandpa told me
        Ghosts eat worms.

We don't eat worms.
We never do.

        We may have germs
        But so do you.

I got here first,
You foolish mouse;
And I'm the one
Who haunts this house.

        I'm not a ghost.
        I don't go BOO!
        But I scare people
        Just like you.

We both scare people!
Yes, we do!

        You needn't be
        Afraid of me.
        I'm just a little thing,
        You see.

And now you know me
So you see
You needn't be
Afraid of me.

        A ghost and mouse are quite a pair!
        We can provide a double scare!
        We'll write some scary stories, too.
        You'll read to me. I'll read to you.

# The Dragon and the Knight

A knight is coming down the street
And he looks good enough to eat.

          **Good enough to eat? Not I!**
          **Dragon, I am thin and dry.**

I don't mind. You'll still taste good.

          **No, I won't! I'm hard as wood.**

Wood is good to chew and gnaw.
I like knights when they are raw.

          **You eat knights? Why, that's disgusting!**
          **Even when our armor's rusting?**

Take it off so I can bite you.

          **No, I need it on to fight you.**

Then I'll eat your armor, too.
There is nothing I can't chew.

          **I will fight you to the death.**

I will burn you with my breath.

          **Help! I think I'm all aflame!**

Aren't you sorry that you came?

          **Dragon, please put out the fire.**
          **If you don't, I will expire.**

If you die, then I'm in luck.
Roasted knight tastes just like duck.

**You're not very well-behaved.
Remember that young girl I saved?**

You mean that damsel in distress?
Yes, you rescued her, I guess.

**I rescued her from you that day.**

And then you took her far away.

**Well, now I'm in distress, you see.
Can't you do the same for me?**

But I'm the one distressing you.
It makes no sense to save you, too.

**But it would be a noble deed.
Would you like to learn to read?**

Learn to read? That would be dreamy.

**I will teach you if you free me.**

There! I've rescued you from me.

**Thank you, Dragon! Now I'm free!**

Let's sit together on this stool
And we'll pretend it's Dragon School.

I'll learn to read.

**And when you're through,**

You'll read to me. I'll read to you.

# The Ghoul

I am a ghoul.

> Why, what's a ghoul?

They didn't teach you
That in school?
A ghoul robs graves
In dark of night.

> Why, that must be
> A scary sight!

It's even worse!
Why, I grow fat
By eating corpses.

> Think of that!

And I do other things
As well.
But they're too terrible
To tell.

> My goodness, ghoul,
> What can they be?

Oh, awful things.

> I'd like to see.

Well, then, you must
Move in with me!

> Move in with you?
> Live with a ghoul?

My ghoul house has
A swimming pool.

Where will I sleep?
What will I eat?

You'll sleep with me.
Our meals are meat.

What kind of meat?

The kind I steal.

I think I'll try
Another meal.
Perhaps a piece
Of plain white bread.

It's tastier
With something dead.

Why, thank you, but
I'd rather not.
A piece of bread
Will hit the spot.

We'll have a picnic
If you wish.

As long as we don't
Share the dish.

And then when both
Of us are through,
You'll read to me,
I'll read to you.

# The Ogre and the Giant

I'm an ogre
Huge and hairy.

I'm a giant
Big and scary.

I am hairier
Than you are.

I am scarier
Than you are.
I'm in lots of
Scary tales.

I'm in lots of
Fairy tales.

People tremble
When they see us.
When they see us,
People flee us.

I do not have
Many friends.

I do not have
Any friends.

Yet we seem to
Like each other.

You could almost
Be my brother.

Would you like to
Be my friend?

Be your friend?
That would depend.
Promise you won't
Beat me up.

Promise you won't
Eat me up.

Eat you? Never!
What a waste!
Well-fed tots
Are to my taste.

Well-fed tots
Stuffed full of cake!
What a dinner
They would make!

Giant, dear,
Since we agree,
Won't you spend
The day with me?

Since it is
Such lovely weather,
Why don't we
Relax together?

Since the day is
Warm and breezy,
Why don't we just
Take it easy?

Stretch out on
The sandy beach.

Take a sunbath.
Eat a peach.

Find a storybook
Or two.
You'll read to me.
I'll read to you.

23

# Scaredy Cats

I hear a shriek.

       I hear a howl.

I hear the hooting
Of an owl.

       I hear the cackle
       Of a witch.

It's very dark.

       It's black as pitch.

I think we're lost.

       I know we are.

I cannot see
A single star.

       I wish that we
       Could see the moon.

I wish that it
Was afternoon.

       I've never seen
       A night so black.

And something's crawling
Down my back.

       And something's creeping
       Up my knee.

     What can they be?
     We cannot see.

Something's coming.
I can hear it.

       Something's coming
       And we're near it.

My feet are sinking
In the muck.

I'm sinking, too.
I think I'm stuck.

I can hardly
Catch my breath.

I am frightened
Half to death.

What a lovely
Way to feel!

Aren't you glad
It wasn't real?

Still, it's great
To feel so gory.
Let's go read
Another story!

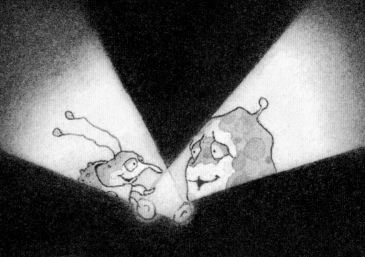

# Trick or Treat

Trick or treat!

Trick or treat!

Wonder what
They'll have to eat!

Hope it's candy!

Hope there's plenty!

Here we are
At number twenty.

Trick or treat!

Trick or treat!

Give us something
Nice and sweet!

Give us something
Nice and quick

Or we'll have to
Play a trick!

Good! It's chocolate!
Chocolate kisses!

Thank you, mister.
Thank you, missus.

Trick or treat!

Trick or treat!

Wait! I'm tripping
On my sheet!

Someone's answering
The bell.

Hope they have
Some caramel!

**One more house.**
**It's getting late.**

Let's just knock
At twenty-eight.

**Trick or treat!**

Trick or treat!

**She says candy's**
**Bad to eat.**

Rots your teeth.
And makes you sick.

**Guess it's time**
**To play a trick!**

Tee hee hee!
That's really icky!

**Tee hee hee!**
**That's really tricky!**

Better run!
The coast is clear!

**Quick!**
**We'd better disappear!**

Hallowe'en
Deserves a cheer!
We can't wait
Until next year!
'Til it comes
What shall we do?
You'll read to me.
I'll read to you.

# Zombies

I'm a zombie.
Who are you?

    Me? I am
    A zombie, too!

Well, we are
A dreadful pair.

    Yes, I know.
    It isn't fair.

People scatter
When they see us.

    Not a person
    Wants to be us.

We are hated.
We are feared.

Well, admit it.
We are weird.

    We are not
    Alive or dead.

We are something else
Instead.

    What a couple.
    What a twosome.

    We scare ourselves,
    We are so gruesome.

Yes, we are.
It's such a pity.

    How I wish
    That we were pretty.

Pretty? That's
Too much to ask.

        Well, we each
        Could wear a mask.

Yes, we could,
And hide our faces.

        Put on costumes,
        Silks, and laces.

Make believe
We're lovely beauties.

        Make believe
        We're charming cuties.

When some passersby
Arrive,

        We'll pretend
        We are alive.

Do not cackle.
Do not squeal.

        Act as if
        We're really real.

Well, we did it!
That was fun!

        We bamboozled
        Everyone!

Let's go home
And just relax.
Have a plate
Of zombie snacks.
Read a zombie
Tale or two.
You'll read to me.
I'll read to you.

# The Phantom

Time for bed.
I'm getting sleepy.
Someone's in here,
Someone creepy.

> Yes, you're right,
> There's someone here.
> You can't see me
> Though I'm near.

Who is speaking?
I can't spy you.

> No, you can't,
> But I'm nearby you.

Are you specter?
Are you spirit?

> No, but you are
> Getting near it.

Can you be a spook
Or ghost?

> You are getting
> Warm as toast.

Well, please tell me.
I can't guess it.

> I'm a phantom,
> I confess it.

Phantoms make me
Quake with fear.
Tell me, are you
Still quite near?

At the place
Where I now stand,
I'm just inches
From your hand.

Can you touch me?
Will I feel?
EEEEEK! I felt you!
You are real!

Yes, I am.
I slide through doors,
Glide through windows,
Walls, and floors.

Wow! I wish
That I were you!
Can I be
A phantom, too?

You a phantom?
Don't be foolish!
Human beings
Can't be ghoulish!
But instead
I wonder whether
We might read
Some tales together?

Scary tales
That really frighten?
They're the ones
That I delight in!

These will make you
Shake, you'll see!
I'll read to you,
You'll read to me.

# The End

The scary stories
Are all done.

We've read them all,
Yes, every one.

We each took turns,
Obeyed the rules,

Pretended we
Were ghosts and ghouls.

We tiptoed over
Squeaky floors.

We visited with
Dinosaurs.

We laughed to hear
A broomstick talking,

Shook to see
A zombie walking.

There are lots more
Scary tales,
Hallowe'en and
Fairy tales,

Tales to hear
And tales to say,

Tales from near
And far away.

Let's go find them,
Old and new.
You'll read to me.
I'll read to you.